Tooth Fairy Trouble

MOLLY MAC

by MARTY KELLEY

PICTURE WINDOW BOOKS
a capstone imprint

This book is dedicated to the real Molly and Kayley.
You two always make me laugh. And to Chris Rose, one
of the most inspiring teachers I've ever met. –Marty

Molly Mac is published by
Picture Window Books
A Capstone Imprint
1710 Roe Crest Drive
North Mankato, MN 56003
www.mycapstone.com

Text © 2017 Marty Kelley
Illustrations © 2017 Marty Kelley

Education Consultant: Julie Lemire
Editor: Shelly Lyons
Designer: Ashlee Suker

Library of Congress Cataloging-in-Publication Data
Names: Kelley, Marty, author, illustrator.
Title: Tooth Fairy trouble / by Marty Kelley;
illustrated by Marty Kelley.
Description: North Mankato, Minnesota: Picture Window Books,
a Capstone imprint, [2017] Series: Molly Mac
Summary: When one of Molly's teeth falls out she prepares for
a visit from the Tooth Fairy, but first she wants to know exactly
what the Fairy does with all those teeth, and whether giving up
one of her teeth is really worth the money she will get—unless it
is at least a million dollars. Identifiers: LCCN 2016043042

ISBN 9781515808381 (library binding)
ISBN 9781515808428 (paperback)
ISBN 9781515808466 (ebook pdf)

Subjects: LCSH: Deciduous teeth–Juvenile fiction. Tooth Fairy
(Legendary character)–Juvenile fiction. Humorous stories.
CYAC: Teeth–Fiction. Tooth Fairy–Fiction.
Humorous stories. LCGFT: Humorous fiction.
Classification: LCC PZ7.K28172 To 2017 DDC [E]–dc23

LC record available at https://lccn.loc.gov/2016043042

Printed and bound in the USA.
010666RP

★ Table of Contents ★

All About Me!

A picture of me!

Name: Molly Mac

People in my family: Mom
Dad
Drooly baby brother Alex

My best friend: KAYLEY!!!!

I really like: Crunchy delicious tacos! But not if they have tomatoes on them. Yuck! They are squirty and wet.

When I grow up I want to be: An artist. And a famous animal trainer. And a professional taco taster. And a teacher. And a super hero. And a lunch lady. And a pirate!

My special memory: Kayley and I camped in my yard. We made s'mores with cheese. They were surprisingly un-delicious.

Chapter 1

The Tape Plan

Zrrrrp. Zrrrrrrrp. Zrrrrrrrrrrrrrrrrp.

Molly pulled out more tape. She carried six swirling strands back to her desk.

"Molly Mac?" asked Kayley.

"Don't ask," mumbled Molly.

"I'm asking," said Kayley.

Molly looked from side to side. She leaned in close to her best friend, Kayley, and whispered, "One of my teeth is loose! I'm afraid it might fall out!"

"But, Molly. . ." said Kayley.

"I'm not going to let it fall out," Molly said. "I'm going to fix it."

She opened her mouth wide. She wrapped a strand of tape over her tooth. It wound around the back of her head. Then she wrapped another, and another, and another. Soon all six shining strands were wound around her tooth and her head.

Mr. Rose strolled over to Molly's desk. He tapped her on the shoulder. "Excuse me, Molly?" he said.

"Don't ask," said Molly.

"I'm asking," replied Mr. Rose.

Chapter 2

Something Got Out!

At lunch, Kayley walked through the noisy lunchroom. She sat down next to the mysterious figure sitting in Molly Mac's regular seat. The figure turned and looked at Kayley.

"Is that you, Molly?" asked Kayley.

"Yes," answered the figure. "Don't ask."

"I'm asking," said Kayley.

"Mr. Rose said no more tape. Ever," replied Molly. "So now if my tooth falls out, I can catch it in this bag. Maybe I'll be able to glue it back in. Where can I get some tooth glue?"

"Teeth fall out, Molly," said Kayley. "It happens to everybody."

Mr. Rose walked past the table. He stopped and looked at the mysterious figure sitting in Molly's spot.

"Molly Mac?" he asked.

Molly gasped. "See, Kayley!" she whispered. "I told you that Mr. Rose has X-ray vision!"

"Do I even want to know why you have a lunch bag on your head?" asked Mr. Rose.

"Probably not," Molly said.

Mr. Rose gently lifted the bag off Molly's head. Molly clapped her hands over her mouth.

"No bags on your head at lunch, Miss Mac," he said, shaking his head. "I've told you that three times this week."

Mr. Rose placed the bag on the table in front of Molly. Then he left to eat his lunch.

"What has gotten into you today?" asked Kayley.

"Nothing has gotten into me," Molly said. She lowered her hands from her mouth. "But something just got out of me." Molly slowly uncurled her fingers. She showed Kayley a small, white tooth lying in her hand.

Molly raced down the hall holding her tooth. She crashed through the bathroom door. Kayley chased after her, calling her name.

"**Ohhhhhhhh,**

noooooooooooo,"

groaned Molly Mac. She looked into the bathroom mirror. She ran her tongue over the space where her tooth had been. "How could this happen to me? I brush my teeth almost every day. Now I look like a pirate."

She held up her tooth and looked at it. "What if all my other teeth fall out, too? I'll look like Grandpa Kevin. He doesn't have **ANY** teeth. All he can eat is pudding!"

Kayley patted Molly's shoulder. "Look on the bright side, Molly," she said. "Now the Tooth Fairy is going to visit!"

Molly clapped her hands over her mouth again. "**NOOOOOOOOOO!!!!!**" she cried. She ran out of the bathroom and headed for the playground.

Chapter 3

Pirate Molly

Molly Mac plopped down on a bench. "I don't want the Tooth Fairy to visit me. What kind of creepy weirdo steals teeth?" she asked.

Kayley sat on the bench next to Molly. "The Tooth Fairy isn't creepy," she answered. "She collects all the teeth kids lose."

Molly raised her eyebrow. "And that sounds normal to you?" she asked. "Who wants a bunch of used teeth? And what does she do with all those teeth?"

"Well, she. . .ummmm. . ." Kayley chewed her lip. "I have no idea," she said.

"This tooth-stealing creep will sneak into my room. Then she will reach under my pillow while I'm asleep! What if she starts collecting eyeballs instead of teeth? I'll have to get an eye patch. Then I'll look even more like a pirate. Why does she collect used teeth?"

"I don't know, Molly," said Kayley. "But I know who can tell us."

After recess, Molly and Kayley raced back to class. They had to talk to Mr. Rose.

"Mr. Rose?" Kayley asked. "What does the Tooth Fairy do with all the teeth she collects?"

"That's a good question, Kayley," he said.

Mr. Rose walked over to his giant bookshelf. He ran his fingers over the books. "Ah, ha!" he exclaimed. "Here it is!" He pulled out a book and opened it. "It says here that some people believe the Tooth Fairy builds her castle with teeth."

"**WHAT? ACK! YUCK!**" Molly yelled. "She builds her house with other people's gross teeth?"

"Well. . ." Mr. Rose said, "I. . .uhhh. . ."

"Is everything in her castle made out of teeth? Her couch? Her bed?" Molly gasped. "Her **TOILET?** Does she have to brush her entire castle every day? Does she have to floss her toaster? How does she make windows out of teeth?"

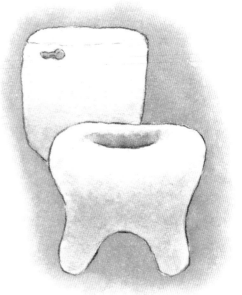

"Well. . ." Mr. Rose loosened his tie. "I. . . uh. . ." He slumped down into his seat. "I have no idea."

Molly walked back to her seat. Kayley sat down beside her.

"It looks like they didn't teach Mr. Rose the really important things in Teacher School," Molly said.

Tap, tap, tap...

Molly drummed her fingers on the table. "I am not letting the Tooth Fairy take my tooth until I find out what she plans to do with it," she told Kayley. "Somebody must know what she does with all those teeth."

Tap, tap, tap...

"**Ah, HA!**" Molly exclaimed. "I've got it! I'll just ask the Tooth Fairy!"

"You can't just talk to the Tooth Fairy," Kayley told her. "Nobody ever sees the Tooth Fairy."

"So, she's invisible?" asked Molly.

"No. It's just that nobody ever sees her," answered Kayley. "She only comes at night."

"Does she bump into things when she flies around at night?" Molly asked. "Or do you think she uses a flashlight? Don't you think people would see her if she has a flashlight?"

"I don't know," said Kayley.

"I'll ask her that, too," Molly said.

"But you can't talk to the Tooth Fairy!" Kayley said.

"Why not? Because she's invisible? Invisible people can talk. Can't they?" Molly asked. "Or are their words invisible, too? Or does she speak another language? I know some French words. **'Oohh, la, la'**. That means, **'wow'** in French."

Kayley shook her head. "No. I mean, yes," she stumbled. "I mean. . .you just can't talk to her. She comes when you're asleep. If you're awake, she doesn't come."

"I know. But how does she know if you're asleep or awake?" asked Molly.

Kayley shrugged. "Magic, I guess," she said.

"I'll do a good job pretending I'm asleep," Molly told her. "She will sneak into my room. Then I can ask her what she does with all the teeth. I'll ask if she needs a flashlight. And I'll ask if she speaks French. I should probably make a list of questions for her."

"I don't think this is going to work," Kayley said.

"Of course it is!" replied Molly. She picked up paper and a pencil from her desk. "It's Friday. You can sleep over, and we will both wait for her. My parents like it when you come over. They say you're a good influence on me."

"Lots of people say that," Kayley replied.

Chapter 4

Molly Mac, Millionaire

Molly Mac burst through her front door.

"**Mom! Dad!**" yelled Molly. "**MOM! DAD!**"

"**SSSSSSHHHHHHHHHH!!!**" her parents both hissed.

Mom closed her laptop. She pointed at the playpen. Molly's baby brother, Alex, was sleeping in it. "Alex is napping," she said. "He's been super cranky all day."

Dad closed his eyes. He flopped back in his chair and started to snore quietly. "I'm sleeping," he whispered. "I have been super cranky all day, too."

Molly held up her tooth. "My tooth fell out!" she shouted.

"That's wonderful!" said Mom.

"It was loose. It fell out because Mr. Rose said no more tape. But now the Tooth Fairy will come to steal it. But it will be dark. And she might not have a flashlight. That would be dangerous, right?"

Dad opened his eyes and sat up. "What are you talking about, Molly?" he asked.

Molly ran over to Dad. She showed him her tooth. "I lost my tooth!"

"No, you didn't," Dad laughed. "It's right in your hand."

Molly sighed and patted Dad's head. "Please don't try to be funny, Dad," she said. "I have told you before. You are not very good at it."

Alex started crying. Mom lifted him out of his playpen. She bounced him gently. "Okay, okay, Mr. Cranky-Pants," she cooed.

Molly held up her tooth. "It fell out at lunch today because Mr. Rose didn't let me use all of the tape. And then he took the bag off my head. Also, Kayley is coming over tonight. We are going to stay awake for the Tooth Fairy. We have some questions to ask her before she sneaks in and steals my tooth. . .and, possibly, my eyeballs, too."

"Questions?" Dad asked. "Like what?"

Molly raised her eyebrow. "Sneaking into rooms at night? Crawling under pillows and stealing used teeth?" Molly answered. "Kayley and I are going to find out what she does with all those teeth."

"I don't know about that, Molly. The Tooth Fairy doesn't come unless you are asleep," Mom said.

"She is not getting my tooth until I find out what she's going to do with it," Molly said. "I don't want her using my tooth as a toaster in her gross castle."

"Ummm, okay," Dad said. "She doesn't steal the teeth, honey. She leaves money under your pillow."

"Money? She leaves money? Why didn't I know that?" Molly asked. She spun her tooth between her fingers. "I'm going to be **RICH!**"

Later that evening, Molly was hard at work in her room.

She didn't hear the phone ring.

She didn't hear someone knocking on the front door.

She didn't hear footsteps coming quickly up the stairs.

Molly Mac was busy.

"Molly?" said Kayley. She opened the bedroom door and walked in.

"Don't ask," Molly said.

"I'm asking," said Kayley.

Molly tapped the piece of paper she was writing on. "I'm making a list of things to buy when I'm rich," she said. "Dad said that the Tooth Fairy leaves money when she takes your tooth. Look at all these great things I'm going to buy!"

Things To Buy When I Am Rich

Automatic taco maker!!

Treehouse with a hot tub full of root beer and a trampoline made out of gummy worms.

A real live unicorn made out of cookie dough.

Molly looked up at her friend. "I'll buy something for you, too!" she said. "What do you want? I'm going to be rich!"

Kayley patted Molly's shoulder. "Thanks, Molly, but I think we need to talk," she said.

Molly put down her pencil. "Okay."

"The Tooth Fairy doesn't bring you millions of dollars," Kayley told her.

"I don't need millions of dollars," Molly said. "One million will be fine."

"I don't think that's going to happen, Molly," Kayley said.

Chapter 5

The Security String

Later that night, Molly Mac stared at the stars on her bedroom ceiling. She rolled over in her sleeping bag and looked at Kayley. "Are you sure the Tooth Fairy isn't going to bring me a million dollars?" she whispered. "I really want that automatic taco maker."

"Sorry, Molly," Kayley said. "The Tooth Fairy doesn't bring you a million dollars."

Molly sighed. She propped herself up on her elbow. "Well, at least we will be able to find out what she does with all the teeth she steals," she said.

"I'm keeping this tooth safe under my pillow until we talk to her. I tied a string to the tooth. And I tied the other end of the string to my big toe." Molly wiggled her toes. "If she tries to take my tooth, it will pull my toe and wake me up! We have to do a good job pretending to sleep, though. Okay, Kayley? Kayley?"

Kayley let out a gentle snore.

"Ohhh, good idea," whispered Molly. She checked the tooth under her pillow one more time. She rolled over and closed her eyes. Then she started to snore.

The next morning, Molly slid out of her sleeping bag. She jumped to her feet. "My tooth!" she cried. "My tooth!" Molly clapped her hands over her eyes. "**Ahhh!**" she cried. "Did she take my eyeballs, too?"

"Wha. . .?" Kayley yawned, rubbing her groggy eyes.

Molly shook Kayley's shoulder. "Kayley! Kayley!" Molly cried. "Are my eyeballs still in my head? My tooth is gone! The Tooth Fairy took it!"

Kayley rolled over. She opened her eyes.

Molly tossed her pillow across the room.
She dropped to her knees and looked for her
tooth. "**My tooth!**" she shouted. "The Tooth Fairy
got my tooth!"

Kayley sat up and groaned.

Molly picked up a long string from the floor. She held it up and looked at her toes. "The Tooth Fairy untied my security string and stole my tooth!" she cried. "And we never even got to talk to her!"

Kayley lifted the corner of Molly's sleeping bag and smiled. "She left you money," she said.

"I don't care about the money!" Molly replied. "I need to know what she's going to do with my tooth! I need to know how she got past my string! I need to know if her toilet is really made of used teeth! She can't use **MY** tooth to build a toilet! Or a toaster!"

Kayley counted the coins. "There's a lot of money here," she said.

"This isn't about the money," Molly said. "Wait a minute. **A LOT** of money? Like, enough for an automatic taco maker?"

"Girls," called Dad, "it's time for breakfast!"

Molly and Kayley hurried down the stairs. They each sat at the kitchen table. Dad put a plate of blueberry pancakes down in front of them.

"So, did you ask the Tooth Fairy what she does with all those teeth?" asked Dad.

"No," Molly sighed. She poured some maple syrup on her pancakes. "She snuck in and stole my tooth before I could ask her. Well, at least she didn't collect my eyeballs instead. That's good!"

"And she left you six quarters!" Kayley said. "That's good, too!"

"Yeah, but I still don't know what the Tooth Fairy does with the teeth she collects," Molly said. "What if she uses my tooth for something awful? I don't want it to become a Tooth Fairy toaster. Or **TOILET**."

"**Ewww...**" Dad and Kayley said together.

"I know, it's **'Ewww'**," Molly cried. "I have to get that tooth back."

Kayley gasped. "You can't get your tooth back! The Tooth Fairy already took it. She left you six quarters."

"I'll give her the quarters back if I have to," Molly said.

"What about the automatic taco maker?" Kayley asked.

Molly shrugged. "I know, but I don't want her using my tooth as a toilet! I'm going to get it back."

"Do I even want to know how you're planning to do that?" asked Kayley.

"Probably not," replied Molly.

After breakfast, Molly Mac marched back up to her room. "What are you doing?" Kayley asked.

"I'm going to find the Tooth Fairy's house," explained Molly. "Then I'm going to knock on the door. I'll tell her I want my tooth back."

Molly stuffed a notebook and some markers in her backpack.

"How will you know which house is hers?" Kayley asked.

"How many giant castles made out of teeth do you think there are?" asked Molly.

"Good point," Kayley admitted. "But what about the money she gave you? You will have to give it back."

Molly sighed. She dumped the six quarters into her backpack. "Yep," she said. "Now I'll never be able to buy that automatic taco maker."

She crammed two stuffed animals and six pairs of socks into her backpack. Next she crammed her piggy bank and a container of leftover pancakes into it, too.

"How long are you going to be gone?" asked Kayley.

"I don't know where the Tooth Fairy lives," Molly said. "I might have to wander all over the entire world searching for her. It could take me a whole hour!"

"What about lunch?" Kayley asked.

"Hmmm. . ." Molly said. "You're right. I should probably bring a sandwich, too."

Chapter 6

Molly's Discovery

Schlrrrp. Molly Mac stood at the kitchen table. She spread grape jelly across a slice of bread. She spread strawberry jam across another slice of bread.

Dad walked into the kitchen. "Molly, why are you making yourself a sandwich? You just ate breakfast."

"I know," Molly said. "But I have big plans."

"Big plans?" asked Dad.

Molly smooshed the two pieces of bread together. "Don't ask," she said.

"I'm asking," he replied.

"I'm going to find the Tooth Fairy and get my tooth back," said Molly.

Dad put the sandwich into a small bag. "And how are you planning to find her?" he asked.

"I'm going to look for the gigantic, nasty castle made of teeth. Have you seen anything like that in our neighborhood?"

Dad scratched his chin. "Not that I can remember," he said.

"I'll ask Mom," Molly said. "Where is she?"

"I'm right here," sang Mom. She swooped into the kitchen carrying Alex. "And look at this!"

Mom and Kayley crowded around Alex. Mom pointed to Alex's mouth full of drool.

"**Whoa**. . ." Molly gasped. "That is gross!"

"It's not gross, Miss Molly," snapped Mom.

"It actually is kind of gross," Kayley said. "I have never seen that much drool in my life!"

"It's Alex's first tooth!" Mom cried. "That's why he has been so cranky."

Molly looked at the small, white crescent on Alex's gum.

"Do you think the Tooth Fairy brought that tooth?" Kayley asked.

"Maybe," Mom said.

Alex squealed. A gooey rope of drool
dripped from his mouth.

Molly's eyes grew wide. "Do you think the Tooth Fairy gave my tooth to Alex? So he can eat crunchy tacos from my automatic taco maker?"

Mom smiled. "It certainly looks like it."

Molly frowned. "I hope she washed it first, because. . .**EWWW**."

Alex gurgled. Another long strand of drool dribbled down his chin.

"Or maybe that's what all the drool's about!" Molly laughed. "Alex is washing the tooth. It's a drool bath."

"So the Tooth Fairy recycles the teeth she collects. Then she gives them to kids who need them?" Kayley said. "That's way smarter than using the teeth to build a castle."

"Yeah," Molly agreed. "Because a tooth castle? Yuck."

Back up in her bedroom, Molly dragged her backpack across the floor.

"This thing is super **HEAVY!**" Molly grunted. She lifted up the backpack and then toppled over. Her backpack thumped to the floor.

Ka-THUNK!

"Looks like you won't need your backpack Molly," Kayley said. "Now you know what the Tooth Fairy does with all of those teeth. You don't need to go find her."

Molly dragged her backpack across the floor. "Not right now," she said. "But I think I'll keep this thing packed, just in case. I may decide to find the Tooth Fairy later. I need to ask her to bring Grandpa Kevin some recycled teeth. He must be getting sick of eating pudding all the time."

"I wouldn't get sick of that!" replied Kayley.

Molly stuffed her backpack into her closet. Then she cleared some art supplies off her desk. She stuffed them in the closet, too.

"What are you doing, Molly?" asked Kayley.

"Making room!" Molly said.

"For what?" Kayley asked.

"Now that I'm not getting my tooth back, I get to keep the money," Molly explained. "So it's time to start saving up for that automatic taco maker."

Molly swept her arm across her desk. The rest of the art supplies crashed to the floor.

"I'm going to put the taco maker right here on my desk!" Molly said. "That way I can have crunchy, delicious tacos for a snack every night."

Mom poked her head in the door. "What was that noise?" she asked. "Molly Mac, do I even want to know what you're doing?"

"Probably not," Molly answered.

All About Me!

A picture of me!

Name:
Marty Kelley

People in my family:
My lovely wife, Kerri
My amazing son, Alex
My terrific daughter, Tori

I really like: Pizza! And hiking in the woods. And being with my friends. And reading. And making music. And traveling with my family.

When I grow up I want to be:
A rock star drummer!

My special memory:
Sitting on the couch with my kids and reading a huge pile of books together.

Find more at my website: www.martykelley.com

MORE
MOLLY MAC

Meet Molly Mac, the curious girl who is always onto something. She's a whirlwind full of questions, and she's out to find the answers!

MOLLY MAC

≥ The Best Friend Bandit ≤
by MARTY KELLEY

MOLLY MAC

≥ Sammy's Great Escape ≤
by MARTY KELLEY

MOLLY MAC

≥ Lucky Break ≤
by MARTY KELLEY

THE FUN
DOESN'T STOP HERE!

Discover more at
www.capstonekids.com

☆ Videos & Contests
☆ Games & Puzzles
★ Friends & Favorites
★ Authors & Illustrators